PJ and His Mouse Go Camping

Lizabeth Danek

PJandhismousebylizabeth.com

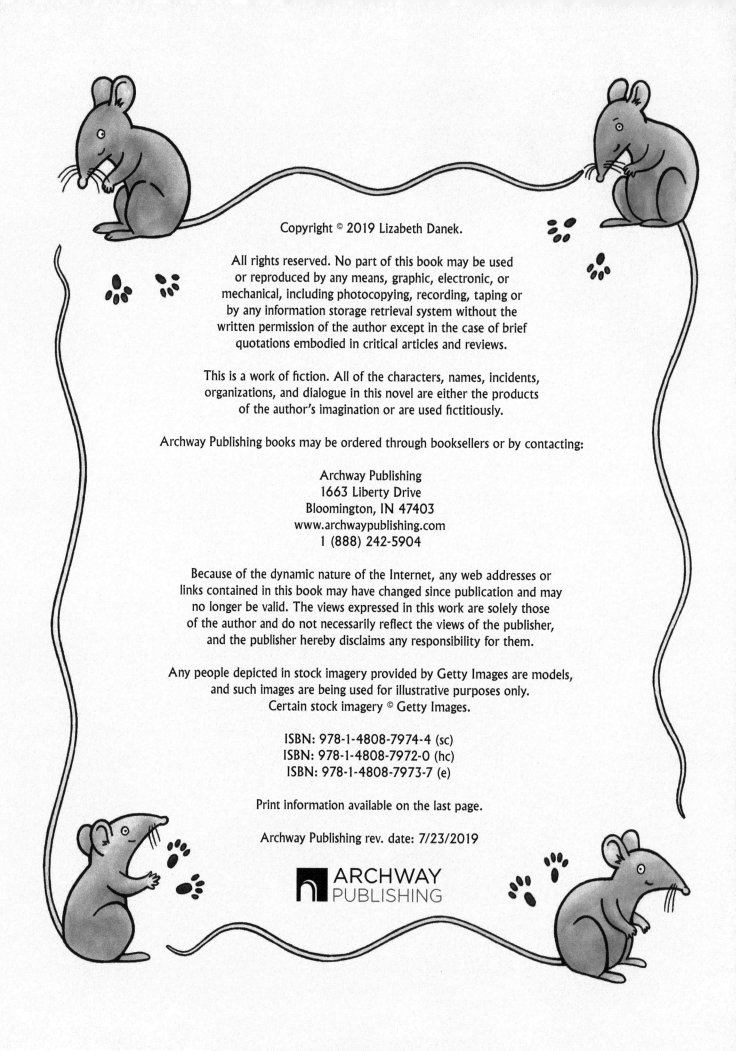

Archway Publishing books may be ordered through booksellers or by contacting:

Archway Publishing
1663 Liberty Drive
Bloomington, IN 47403
www.archwaypublishing.com
1 (888) 242-5904

ISBN: 978-1-4808-7974-4 (sc)
ISBN: 978-1-4808-7972-0 (hc)
ISBN: 978-1-4808-7973-7 (e)

Print information available on the last page.

Archway Publishing rev. date: 7/23/2019

ARCHWAY
PUBLISHING

PJ is a little boy who
lives with his family in
a house in the city.

PJ and his friends like to play. Most days they like to play stickball in the street.

One day while playing stickball in the street, the Moms yell from the front steps, "Let's go camping!"

All the children scream "Hooray!". They gather their bats, balls and baseball gloves so the mean old tomcat who crouches in the gutters and alleys doesn't snatch them in his dirty old claws.

And the families are off! PJ with his mouse, Julie with her mole, and friends, JT and Tammy, the twins.

Everyone helps set up camp.

The next morning all the families eat breakfast around the campfire.

JT and Tammy, the twins, like to watch the fire. They sit, they think and sometimes they feel sad.

After breakfast by the fire, everyone goes on a hike. PJ and his mouse, Julie and her mole, JT and Tammy run in front.

PJ and his mouse, Julie and her mole, JT and Tammy, the twins, find big sticks to carry on their hike through the woods.

A mom chipmunk and her baby are stuck in a log. Two fang-toothed snakes are slithering toward the chipmunks stuck in the log. Rattling their rattles and gnashing their fangs.

JT, Tammy, PJ and Julie don't know what to do.

PJ's mouse and Julie's
mole do! They jump from
PJ's shoulder and Julie's
hat and circle the snakes.

Running faster and faster in circles around the fang-toothed snakes until the snakes are tied in knots.

JT and Tammy rush in and using their sticks, push the dizzy snakes tied in knots away from the log.

They free the chipmunks from the log and the chipmunks are happy to be safe.

JT and Tammy bring the chipmunks back to camp in their backpacks and bandage their legs.

They sit by the fire and share their roasted marshmallows and juice.

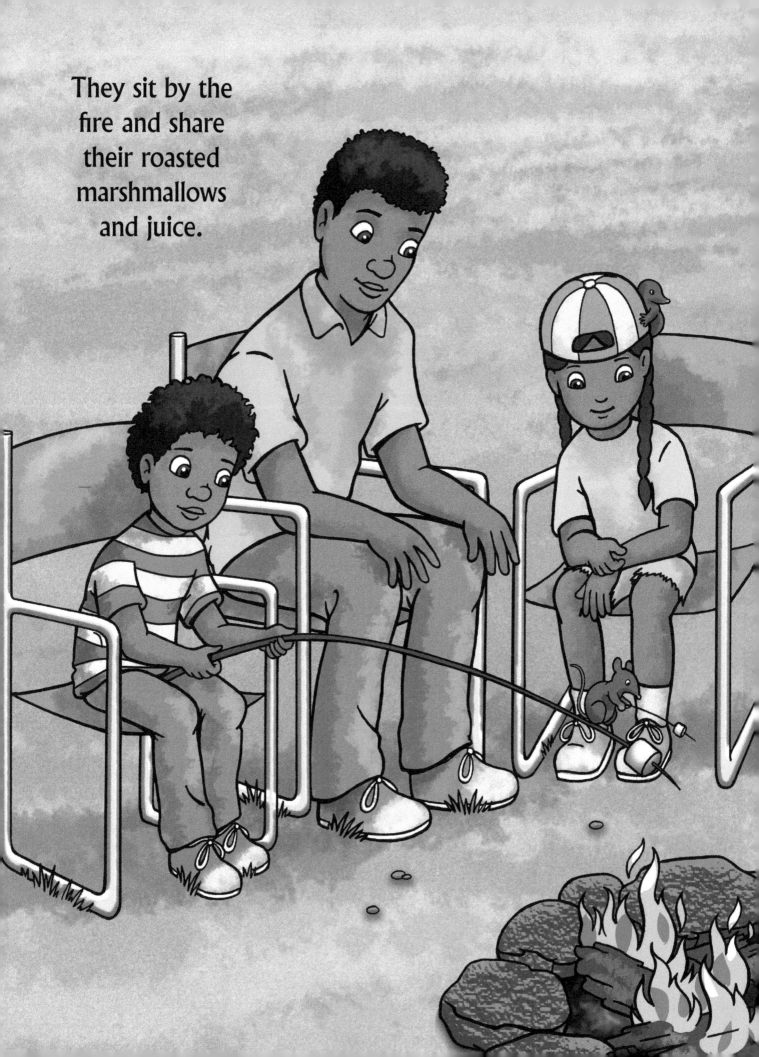

The next day it is time to go back to the city.

JT and Tammy set the chipmunks down
to join their forest friends.

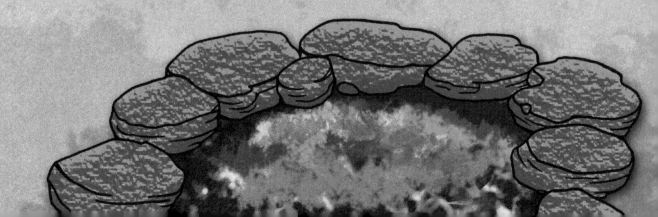

But, the chipmunks don't run off!

Instead they bring their forest friends to meet JT and Tammy. The forest friends are happy to see them safe!

All the families are ready to go. JT and Tammy, the twins, PJ and his mouse, Julie and her mole all get into the car and head home.

Then to everyone's surprise the chipmunk and her baby jump out of the backpack and into JT and Tammy's lap!

They are all going back to the city!

Now when PJ and his mouse, Julie and her mole, JT and Tammy and their chipmunks sit on the steps in the city, they sit, they think, and they feel happy!

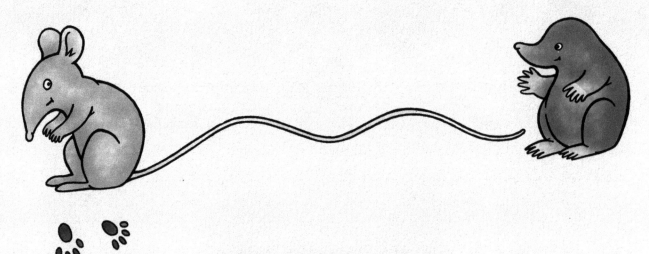

QUESTIONS FOR
THE READER

- Do you think what JT and Tammy did was kind?
- Do you think what PJ's mouse and Julie's mole did was brave?
- Do you think they learned from PJ and Julie how to be kind?
- Can you share when you've been kind to someone? How did that make you feel? How did it make them feel?
- What is one thing can you do today to be kind to someone you know?

CPSIA information can be obtained
at www.ICGtesting.com
Printed in the USA
BVHW021059080819
555410BV00015B/291/P